The Relatives Came

Story by CYNTHIA RYLANT

Illustrated by STEPHEN GAMMELL

Atheneum Books for Young Readers
New York   London   Toronto   Sydney

ATHENEUM BOOKS FOR YOUNG READERS
An imprint of Simon & Schuster Children's Publishing Division
1230 Avenue of the Americas, New York, New York 10020
Text copyright © 1985 by Cynthia Rylant
Illustrations copyright © 1985 by Stephen Gammell
ATHENEUM BOOKS FOR YOUNG READERS is a registered trademark of Simon & Schuster, Inc. For information about special discounts for bulk purchases, please contact Simon & Schuster Special Sales at 1-866-506-1949 or business@simonandschuster.com. The Simon & Schuster Speakers Bureau can bring authors to your live event. For more information or to book an event, contact the Simon & Schuster Speakers Bureau at 1-866-248-3049 or visit our website at www.simonspeakers.com.
Also available in an Atheneum Books for Young Readers hardcover edition.
The text for this book is set in 16 pt. Benguiat Book Condensed.
The illustrations for this book are rendered in colored pencil, reproduced in full color.
Manufactured in China
1 1 1 1   SCP
First Atheneum Books for Young Readers paperback edition July 1993
40 39 38 37 36 35 34 33

The Library of Congress has cataloged the hardcover edition as follows:
Rylant, Cynthia.
The relatives came / story by Cynthia Rylant; illustrated by Stephen Gammell. – 1st ed.
p.   cm.
Summary: The relatives come to visit from Virginia and everyone has a wonderful time.
ISBN 978-0-689-84508-6 (hc)
(1. Family life—Fiction.) I. Gammell, Stephen, ill. II. Juvenile Collection (Library of Congress) III. Title.
PZ7.R982Re   1996
(E)—dc20 92-41394
ISBN 978-0-689-71738-3 (pbk)

For Aunt Agnes Little and her brood,

Dick Jackson and his, Gerry and ours

It was in the summer of the year when the relatives came. They came up from Virginia. They left when their grapes were nearly purple enough to pick, but not quite.

They had an old station wagon that smelled like a real car,
and in it they put an ice chest full of soda pop
and some boxes of crackers and some bologna sandwiches,
and up they came—from Virginia.

They left at four in the morning when it was still dark,
before even the birds were awake.

They drove all day long and into the night, and while they

traveled along they looked at the strange houses

and different mountains and they thought

about their almost purple grapes back home.

They thought about Virginia—

but they thought about us, too. Waiting for them.

So they drank up all their pop
and ate up all their crackers
and traveled up all those miles until finally
they pulled into our yard.

Then it was hugging time. Talk about hugging!

Those relatives just passed us all around their car, pulling us

against their wrinkled Virginia clothes, crying sometimes.

They hugged us for hours.

Then it was into the house and so much laughing
and shining faces and hugging in the doorways.
You'd have to go through at least four different hugs
to get from the kitchen to the front room. Those relatives!

And finally after a big supper two or three times around
until we all got a turn at the table, there was quiet talk
and we were in twos and threes through the house.

The relatives weren't particular about beds, which was good
since there weren't any extras, so a few squeezed in with us
and the rest slept on the floor, some with their arms
thrown over the closest person, or some with an arm across one person
and a leg across another.

It was different, going to sleep with all that new breathing in the house.

The relatives stayed for weeks and weeks. They helped us
tend the garden and they fixed any broken things they could find.

They ate up all our strawberries and melons,

then promised we could eat up all their grapes and peaches

when we came to Virginia.

But none of us thought about Virginia much. We were so busy hugging and eating and breathing together.

Finally, after a long time, the relatives loaded up their ice chest
and headed back to Virginia at four in the morning.
We stood there in our pajamas and waved them off in the dark.
　We watched the relatives disappear down the road,
then we crawled back into our beds that felt too big and too quiet.
We fell asleep.

And the relatives drove on, all day long and into the night,
and while they traveled along they looked
at the strange houses and different mountains
and they thought about their dark purple grapes
waiting at home in Virginia.

But they thought about us, too. Missing them. And they missed us.

And when they were finally home in Virginia,
they crawled into their silent, soft beds and dreamed
about the next summer.

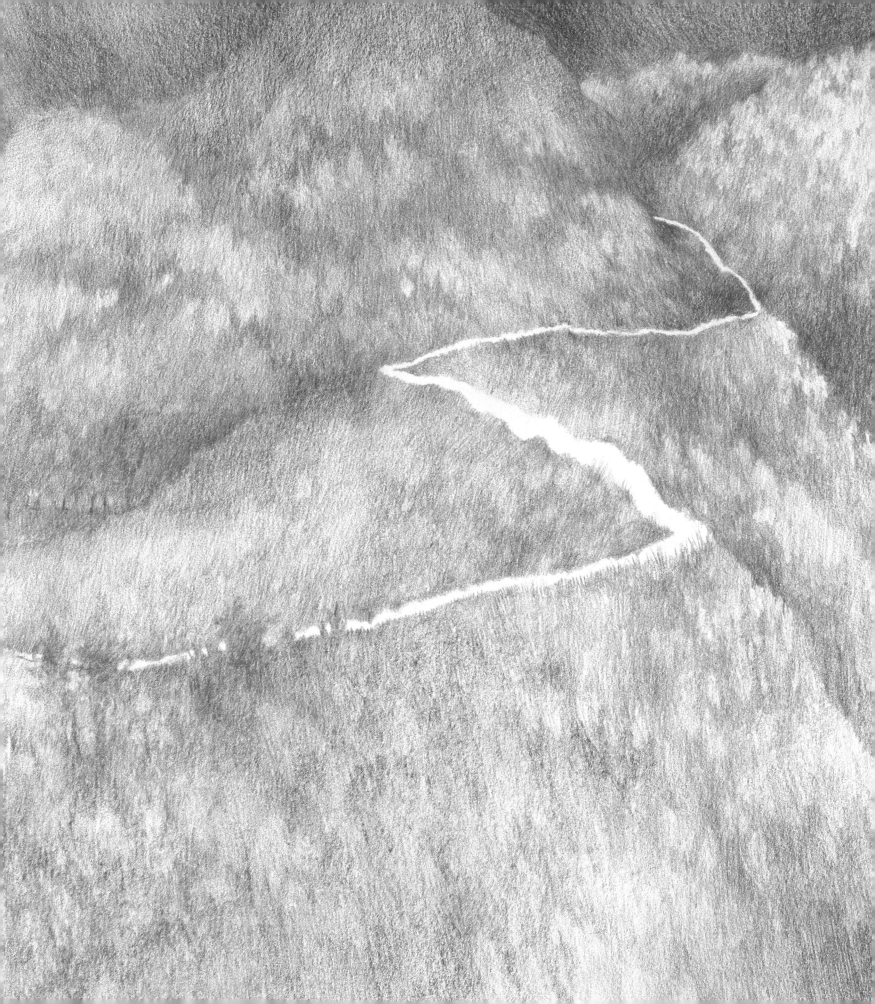